JESSIE'S ISLAND

Orca Book Publishers

Written by Sheryl McFarlane

Illustrated by Sheena Lott

JESSIE'S ISLAND

Dear Jessie,

You must be awfully bored living on an island in the middle of nowhere. There's all kinds of things to do here, like . . . hockey, tennis, swimming, soccer, going to the zoo, video games at the mall, eating out and then catching a movie or a concert. And if it's cold or snowing, the planetarium or museum are fun, and the science centre is sure to have something new.

"I guess we'd better invite your cousin Thomas for a visit, Jessie."

Dear Thomas,

If you come to my island,

I will show you . . .

the bald eagles that summer in our giant fir tree,

and the curious harbour seals that pop their slippery, whiskered faces up when we swim to the raft that Dad built.

And even on the grayest winter day, we can
watch for killer whales travelling up the strait,

or maybe we'll see a lone minke whale breech-feeding,

and there's a shy otter family we can see if we
paddle very quietly in the canoe.

There are so many birds to see, especially in spring . . .

oyster catchers,   plovers,   sandpipers   and gulls,

kingfishers,   coots,   mergansers,

herons   and loons,

and harlequins so pretty, they look painted.

We'll explore the abandoned cabin where the
trees grow through the roof.

and climb up to the point to watch the ferries
pass so close it seems they could crash, except they
never do.

We'll throw sticks into the swirling, frothy water just to watch them disappear or break up on the jagged rocks

and peel strips of red arbutus bark until the trunk
is silky smooth and we can slither down like snakes.

We'll pick huckleberries in mid-summer and

blackberries in fall.

But my very, very favourite are the tiny wild strawberries of early spring.

We can fish for salmon, jig for cod, dig for clams
and set the crab trap in the bay.

We'll have fights with giant ribbons of slippery kelp, and . . .

I'll show you purple starfish clinging to the rocks
and anemonies with pink feathery tentacles that
close up if you put your fingers near

and periwinkles that move so slow, you can
hardly tell they've moved at all

and tiny hermit crabs toting empty shells to hide in.

And when you come to visit my island,
Thomas, you might never, ever want to
leave.

From your cousin,
Jessie.

To my husband, for dragging me up that first mountain, and to
Ali, Cloe and Katie, for rekindling a deep love of nature's beauty.
S.M.

To all parents who instill a love of reading in their children,
and to my own family — Nick, Nathan, Fraser and Chelsea.
S.L.

Text Copyright © 1992 Sheryl McFarlane
Illustrations Copyright © 1992 Sheena Lott

Publication assistance provided by The Canada Council.
All rights reserved.

First printing, 1992
Second printing, 1993
Third printing, 1993
Fourth printing, 1994

Orca Book Publishers
PO Box 5626 Stn B
Victoria, BC Canada
V8R 6S4

Orca Book Publishers
PO Box 468
Custer, WA USA
98240-0468

Design by Christine Toller
Printed in Hong Kong

Canadian Cataloguing in Publication Data
McFarlane, Sheryl, 1954–
Jessie's island
ISBN 0-920501-76-1

I. Lott, Sheena, 1950– II. Title
PS8575.F37J6 1992   jC813'.54   C92-091106-4
PZ7.M233Jo 1992